THE OWL FAMILY AND NICODEMUS MEET JESUS

Margaret A. Marshall

Illustrations by: Eumir Carlo Fernandez

LIGHT TO MY LAMP BOOKS

To order additional copies of this book, contact:
Xlibris Corporation
1-888-795-4274
www.Xlibris.com
Orders@Xlibris.com

DEDICATED TO MY GRANDCHILDREN

Luke

Ben

Xavier

Nina

Madeline

Sam

INTRODUCTION

THE OWL FAMILY AND NICODEMUS MEET JESUS. The owl family meets to discuss their encounters with Jesus. Of course, owls don't really talk to us, but they can talk with each other. Did they exist? We will never know, but we do know God exists. We know that Jesus exists. We know that the Holy Spirit exists.

Parts of the story are written in the Bible. The rest of the story is made up to help you learn about Jesus. Imagine what Jesus is saying to you.

THE OWL FAMILY AND NICODEMUS MEET JESUS is the second book in the Meet Jesus series that I have written for my grandchildren. For further information, contact me at lighttomylamp@live.com. You can visit my website www.margaretamarshall.com.

CONTENTS

THE OWL FAMILY

The owl family, six in number, awoke from a day's sleep. Mom and Pop plus four baby owls lived in a tree. Pop stood firm and fair and consistent while Mom wavered a bit, but she was most loving. The children—named Lukey, Ben, Mattie, and Sammy—looked like most owls. Their faces, round like satellite dishes or reflectors, collect and focus sound waves. Their feathers, so soft, muffle the sounds they make when approaching their prey.

Lukey, the firstborn and the biggest owlet, considered himself the oldest and the wisest. He liked to tell the others what to do and how to do it. Mom and Pop called him Lukey the Leader.

His brother, Ben, accepted Lukey's dare by flying onto some campers' tent, hissing and screaming, to wake them. Mom questioned, "How can an owl get into so much mischief?"

"He's lucky the Lord let him live," Pop added.

Mom and Pop called Ben, because of his daring actions, Benny the Bold. If Lukey the Leader dared Benny the Bold to wake the neighborhood, Ben would obey. To look at Ben, one would think he was shy since he continually looked downward.

Mattie, the third oldest, appreciated her good looks. If she disappeared from her parents' sight, she could be found near a pond. She loved looking at her reflection in the water on a moonlit evening. Once she found a yellow feather and stuck it into her own soft feathers. She liked it so well, she still wears a colorful feather. Mom and Pop called her Mattie the Moonlighter since she loved the moonlight.

Finally, Sammy, the cutest little owl, made his appearance. You could tell him apart from the rest of the family by his slanted eyes. The happiest in the bunch, he cheered the entire family day after day just by his smile. Mom and Pop called him Sammy Sunshine since no other words could describe how he made the family feel. Besides, he liked being awake during the daylight and asleep during the night when most owls stay awake.

UNCLE CHARLEY

I'm Uncle Charley. I'm Pop's brother. I fly over to the family's tree from time to time. Let me tell you a little about myself and the rest of the family. We are barn owls. We like to nest in hollow trees, but we may nest in caves, buildings, or niches in cliffs. We eat rodents—little animals that are harmful to crops. We swallow them whole. The bones come up later.

Most owls spend the night searching for food though we can see well in the daylight. Sammy knows that. Our eyes aren't any better than yours in the darkness, but our hearing is very acute. That is, it's very sharp. We locate our prey by sound. Our faces help us because of the shape. You can't see our ears because they are hidden under our feathers.

Quite often we meet in my brother's family tree in the early evening. Today we met on a large boulder in the dark afternoon. We heard of the death of our friend, Jesus, so we made the trip to show our respects. We watched Jesus's friend, Nicodemus, bring herbs and spices to his tomb. Tears flowed while they placed Jesus in his grave.

I met Jesus during a celebration called the Feast of Booths, the annual feast of thanksgiving for the fall harvest. The Israelites celebrated the pillar of fire leading their relatives through the desert to the promised land. They remembered how Moses brought water out of a rock when the people complained of their thirst while in the desert.

Just in case you don't remember, I'll remind you. Very many years ago, the Israelites lived in Egypt. They were made slaves. God picked Moses to lead the Israelites to a land he promised them where they wouldn't have to be slaves. On the way, they wandered in the desert. They complained they were hungry so the Lord sent manna and quail for them to eat. Then they complained they were thirsty. The Lord told Moses to strike his rod on the rock and water burst forth.

After a very long time, a pillar of fire led the Israelites out of the desert. Now they are living in the promised land, Israel. That's where we are living.

UNCLE OWL MEETS JESUS

I happened to be napping in a nook in the temple when I heard Jesus proclaiming, "If anyone thirst, let him come to me and drink. He who believes in me, as the scripture has said, 'Out of his heart shall flow rivers of living water.'"

I put two and two together. The Celebration of Booths recalled Moses striking the rock and giving the Israelites water. Now Jesus offered living water for all who came to him.

Jesus sensed that I believed. He looked up and said, "Through your belief, the Holy Spirit will accomplish great things in your life. Uncle Owl, Lukey, Ben, Mattie, and Sammy need you."

I heard people saying, "This is really the prophet." Others said, "This is the Christ." Some said, "Is the Christ to come from Galilee? Has not the scripture said that the Christ comes from Bethlehem?"

Some of the people didn't believe Jesus to be the savior. The Pharisees and chief priests sent officers to arrest Jesus, but no one did.

When the soldiers that had been sent reported to the chief priests and Pharisees without Jesus, they were asked, "Why did you not bring him?"

The officers replied, "No man ever spoke like this man!"

The Pharisees answered, "Have you been fooled like the rest who do not know the law?"

A man named Nicodemus, one of the Pharisees, said, "Does our law judge a man without first giving him a hearing and learning what he does?"

They taunted, "Are you from Galilee too? Search and you will see that no prophet is to rise from Galilee."

After Jesus left the temple without being arrested, I met him again. He looked up to where I was perched and said, "We both escaped. It wasn't our time yet. My time is near, but you must go on to fulfill God's will for you."

I flew over to my brother's family tree to tell them what I saw and heard.

THE OWLS SHARE ENCOUNTERS

When I reached my brother's family tree, I told them that I had met Jesus, the son of God. They told me a while back about meeting Jesus, but I didn't pay much attention. Now I wanted to hear the story again.

My brother said, "Jesus and his disciples camped under our home one night. They prayed. Jesus recited a line and the apostles answered:

Praise the Lord, who is so good.
God's love endures forever.
Praise the God of gods;
God's love endures forever.
Praise the Lord of lords;
God's love endures forever.

"After discussing the day's activities, most of them fell asleep. A man called Peter snored loudly.

"Even though we kept quiet, Jesus started to talk to us. He said, 'You have a fine family.' He told the children how special they were and how he loved them.

"'Lukey,' he said, 'You are a leader and you need to use that leadership to do good things and not get your brother into trouble.'

"He told Ben, 'Boldness is a good thing. Use it for good. Think before you act. Put yourself in your neighbor's place.'

"He looked at Mattie and said, 'You are a very pretty owl. Remember that your beauty is God's gift to you but more important is the beauty that is inside your soul. What you do with your life will bring you back to me.'

"To Sammy, Jesus said, 'Sammy, you are a beautiful owl. Your smile shows your beauty within. Keep thinking good thoughts!'

"'Mom and Pop,' Jesus said, 'You are doing fine with your children!'

"Before the children could react, a man approached. Jesus said, 'Now listen. A man named Nicodemus is approaching. He is a ruler of the Jews. Listen!'

"We all nodded our heads and sat quietly and listened.

"'Rabbi,' Nicodemus said, 'We know you are a teacher come from God, for no man can perform signs and wonders such as you perform unless God is with him.'

"Jesus answered, 'Truly, truly, unless a man is born anew, he cannot see the kingdom of God.'

"Nicodemus asked, 'How can a man be born when he is old? Can he enter a second time into his mother's womb and be born?'

"Jesus said, 'Truly, truly, I say to you, unless one is born of water and the spirit, he cannot enter the kingdom of God. That which is born of the flesh is flesh and that which is born of the spirit is spirit.'"

Uncle Owl interrupted Pop's story, "Living water! Living water!"

Pop's eyes widened as he continued with a joyful screech.

"Nicodemus asked, 'How can this be?'

20

"Jesus responded, 'You are a teacher of Israel and still you do not understand this? If I tell you earthly things and you do not believe, how can you believe if I tell you heavenly things? No one has ascended into heaven but he who descended from heaven, the Son of Man. And as Moses lifted up the serpent in the wilderness, so must the Son of Man be lifted up, that whoever believes in me may have eternal life.'"

Pop said, "Nicodemus looked puzzled as he walked away. Since the night was quickly passing and the children couldn't keep quiet any longer, we flew away so Jesus could get some sleep. When we all perched on a tree, questions flowed. 'What was Jesus talking about? Who's Moses?'

"Mom explained to the children about Moses leading the Israelites in the desert. She told them how God picked Moses to lead the Israelites from Egypt where they were slaves and how they spent time in the desert.

"She said, 'They developed an attitude and forgot about God.' He wanted to remind them that he had their best interest at heart so he sent snakes and they were getting bitten. Finally they asked for help. The Lord told Moses to make a bronze snake, put it on the pole, and look at it. When they looked at the snake, believing what God said, they were healed. Their faith returned, and they were safe.'

"'God wants us to believe and trust him,' Luke exclaimed.

"Still thinking about what Jesus told Nicodemus, Ben raised his eyes and asked, 'What's eternal life?'

"'You will live forever,' I explained.

"Mattie looked puzzled. 'You said we could die if we are not careful!'

"Mom tilted her head and spoke tenderly, 'Someday our life on this earth will end, but we will live with Jesus forever in heaven. That's where he came from and will go back soon.'

"Sammy's smile disappeared. He cried, 'Jesus is leaving?'"

Pop closed his eyes and thought about Jesus's words. "Remember Jesus told Nicodemus that he is going back to heaven, but he is going to send the Holy Spirit to help us."

All the little owls asked at once, "Holy Spirit?"

I questioned, "Did you tell them the Holy Spirit is Jesus's love within them—like living water?"

Pop said, "I sure did. I reminded the children that the Holy Spirit will help them become the good owls God wants them to be. I pointed to the river and said, 'Look at that fresh clear water. That is living water. Now look at that muddy water in the puddle. That water just sits there until it disappears.'"

Mom quietly, but with great concern, added, "We talked about Moses putting the bronze snake on the pole and wondered why he compared himself to the snake on the pole. I do know that he wants us to believe in him."

I answered, "I know we will find out soon."

THE OWLS' QUESTIONS
ARE ANSWERED

Now the day has come and Jesus has suffered and died on the cross. With tears in our eyes and love in our hearts, we, seven in number, discussed Jesus's words.

Mom whispered softly, "I understand why Jesus told Nicodemus that he would be lifted up as Moses lifted up the serpent in the wilderness."

"Yes," I, Uncle Charley, responded. "The Lord wanted to give the people a sign of healing. When they looked at it and believed God would take care of them, they lived."

"Jesus was raised up on the cross to save us too," Ben added.

Mattie cried, "I miss him already!"

Lukey tried to console Mattie by reminding her of Jesus's promise that he would always be in our hearts. "Jesus will return to heaven and send the Holy Spirit to be with us."
Pop reminded us that the Holy Spirit will be as alive in us as the water that runs through the Jordan River from Mount Hermon.

"Living water, living water," I screeched as I flapped my wings.

Little Sammy beamed with delight. "The Holy Spirit will help us be the owls Jesus wants us to be."

Pop proudly said, "All our questions are answered. We believe. That's why people say owls are wise."

MANY, MANY YEARS LATER

All the owls were baptized.

Luke the Leader led his brothers and sister on the path to righteousness. That is, they are on their road to heaven. Each one looks up to him for advice and assistance.

Ben the Bold reveals his bravery in showing Jesus's love to all. He always thinks about the words of Jesus: "Do unto others as you would want them to do to you."

Mattie the Moonlighter still is a moonlight lover. Her eyes shine like the light of a full moon because of the love in her heart. She still perches on a tree next to the water, but now she meditates and dwells on the living water, the Holy Spirit.

Sammy Sunshine smiles continually as he brings love into other's hearts when he tells them about Jesus.

Mom and Pop left this earth for a more peaceful site. I am getting ready to meet Jesus in heaven, but for now, Jesus wants me to finish my assignment and this is it. Now you work on yours!

Uncle Owl

Printed in the USA
CPSIA information can be obtained
at www.ICGtesting.com
CBHW040524100924
14332CB00002B/20